Fritzy Finds a Hat

A gentle tale to help talk
with children about cancer

by Scott Hamilton

with Mary Coffeen

Illustrated by Brad Paisley

with Bill Kersey

Acknowledgments

This book was made possible by many people who have been directly impacted by cancer.

Thank you, Brad Paisley, for creating beautiful artwork that
captures a young boy's desire to help his mother.

Thank you, Mary Coffeen and Moffitt Cancer Center, for getting this book off the ground.
This story has been yours to share as you work tirelessly to change our world.

Jonathan Merkh has been incredibly supportive to represent this book in the publishing world. Thank
you for making sure Fritzy gets into every household that needs these words to help those we love.

Thank you, Bill Kersey, for your art direction and getting Fritzy, his mom, and her hats through this story.

A huge amount of appreciation to Carrie Simons and Triple7 PR for everything
she does to make a difference at CARES and for the cancer community.

Thanks to Karri Morgan for working so diligently to get this project to the
finish line. Your love for others is obvious in everything you do.

Fritzy Finds a Hat: A gentle tale to help talk with children about cancer

Copyright © 2020 by Scott Hamilton CARES Foundation and H. Lee Moffitt Cancer Center & Research Institute, Inc.

Photo credit: Jeff Lipsky
Photo credit: Kathryn Costello

ISBN: 9781948677400 print
ISBN: 9781948677417 ebook
Printed in China
First edition, February 2020

Dedication

This book is dedicated to everyone in the battle against cancer, including caregivers, family, and those trying to make a difference in the cancer community through research.

For Dorothy, my mom, who fought and lost her battle against cancer over 40 years ago. Her battle was valiant and taught a young boy not only how to live, but to eventually fight and defeat his own cancer.

It was a Tuesday, and Fritzy Goldwing started his morning with a very important assignment. He had to find the perfect hat for his mom.

"It has to be **THE BEST,** the bestest best!" Fritzy announced, tying up his skates to begin the search.

"Something that makes her smile, like when I finish my broccoli."

"Or maybe it makes her laugh — laugh so hard she gets hiccups!"

Fritzy needed the right hat **FAST** because this was going to be his new job on Tuesdays – picking out the perfect hat for his mom's trip to the hospital.

Fritzy's mom had cancer.
That was a scary word,
and he knew it meant
mommy was sick.
But she sat him down, and with
a great big hug, she shared what
the doctor had told her.

It wasn't something he could catch, and it wasn't something he had caused, but she would have to take some very strong medicine to help her body get better. Sometimes, she wouldn't feel so good... and there was one **BIG** surprise – the medicine might make her hair fall out!

"Mommy says hair grows back,"
Fritzy explained to his cat Percy,
"but having a few new hats will
make the time go faster".

So Fritzy, who never did anything slow, used his skates to help him go faster! Fritzy loved to skate more than anything... more than peanut butter and jelly maybe. And skating fast helped him think even quicker.

"What would Mommy like today?," he wondered, practicing his figure eights around Wimpole, the tiny town where he was born.

First, he thought about a hat with pillows. "One on each side, so Mommy can rest when she gets tired," Fritzy explained, remembering the medicine would make her sleepy.

"Or maybe a hat with a phone?"
Fritzy knew his mom loved to keep
in touch, even if she would be home
before it was time to tuck him in.

"Or she might like a furry hat to keep her warm," Fritzy said, noting that Percy would be "purr-fect", because sometimes the hospital can be very cold.

"I could find a hat with hugs and kisses so she knows I'm always there, even if I can't come along…"

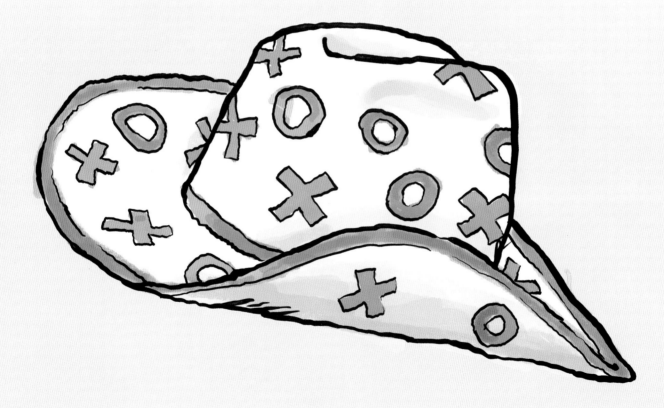

"But she might like a soup-and-crackers hat just in case her tummy gets rumbly." Her doctor said she might not eat much.

"And here's my favorite," said Fritzy.
"A hat filled with jokes ('knock, knock...')!
THAT will make her hiccup!!"

Fritzy thought and thought, and skated and skated...and he even slowed down a bit to say a little prayer, because that always made him feel better and maybe it would help his mom feel better too.

Suddenly, Fritzy jumped for joy.
He had an idea.
An idea that made him flip
– an upside down flip!

Fritzy found the perfect hat,
the best hat of all.
One that he made
all by himself.

"Mommy said it was the **BEST**, the very bestest best," Fritzy said, beaming with pride.

And not because it was funny or furry
or filled with her favorite jokes.
It reminded her of Fritzy,
his mom said,
and that was
the best gift of all.

Proceeds from *Fritzy Finds A Hat* will benefit vital cancer research through the Scott Hamilton CARES Foundation and at Moffitt Cancer Center, as well as Moffitt's Families First Program.

Scott Hamilton is a New York Times best-selling author, an Olympic Gold Medalist, cancer survivor, broadcaster, motivational speaker, husband, father and eternal optimist. The Scott Hamilton CARES Foundation is dedicated to changing the future of cancer by funding advanced, innovative research that treats the cancer while sparing the patient. Scott lives in Nashville with his beautiful wife, Tracie, and their four amazing children.

Brad Paisley is a critically acclaimed singer, songwriter, guitarist, entertainer and artist whose talents have earned him numerous awards, including three GRAMMYs, two American Music Awards, 14 Academy of Country Music Awards and 14 Country Music Association Awards, among many others.

The Families First program at Moffitt Cancer Center helps families and their children adjust to the many changes that occur when a parent has cancer. Education, preparation and support help families cope successfully when facing a serious illness. Located in Tampa, Florida, Moffitt is a National Cancer Institute-designated Comprehensive Cancer Center. Scott Hamilton is a member of its national Board of Advisors.